Best Friend's Girl

By: Alexander Martin

Copyright 2023 Alexander Martin

Author Note:

This is a work of fiction, none of the characters are real or are they based on real people or events. Please do not take the actions or expressions noted in this story as the Author's outlook on life or respected behavior of anybody alive or deceased.

Please have fun and enjoy reading these stories.

Chapter One: The Girl

"**S**hit!" I said quickly, getting out of bed. I was late; technically, I was still early for work, but with all the other things I wanted to do today. I was running a bit late.

Quickly springing out of bed, I gathered my morning workout bag and headed for the shower. As usual, it was locked.

"Dammit, Chris!" I yelled at my roommate.

He was always holding up the bathroom for hours on end.

"Sorry, Martin," I heard from behind the door.

He was a good friend; well, he was my best friend.

Chris and I had been friends since before high school, well over ten years ago. But he was such a pretty boy. We had come to the big city together many years ago. We decided it was best to stick together until we were ready to go it alone.

I didn't know then that he would take up over two hours in the bathroom.

"Nearly finished," he said as the door opened. "Done."

His blonde hair was spiked with enough gel to make a male model jealous. He always wore skin-tight clothes, which today was no different.

"One of these days I am going to buy you a skirt!" I shouted down the hall.

"Then he will be wearing mine," a voice said behind me.

"Morning Roxy," I said as I quickly launched myself into the bathroom before she could go in.

I quickly got changed for the gym.

Taking a glance into the mirror. I still looked the same as in high school, maybe a little heavier. Six feet five inches tall, with dark black skin. I shaved my head weekly and kept a shaved face. With a mustache, everything was neatly trimmed.

I worked out daily, so I was probably in the best shape of my life, with low body fat, shaved head, and dark brown eyes.

I was okay with the way I looked and opened the door.

Roxy stood there with her arms folded and yawning. She was Chris's girlfriend.

They had been dating for just under a year now. Chris said she would only stay with us for a few weeks, but it was four months now. Not that I was complaining; she was eye candy, and by eye candy, I meant every sense of the word.

She had fire-red hair, emerald green eyes, a tight five-foot-six-inch frame, long shapely legs, and a nice ass. But Roxy's main attribute was her chest. They were huge, not just huge. They were on the verge of being humongous. On her tall but medium-sized body, they looked even more enormous. I knew exactly how big they were, which didn't help.

One day one of her bras was lying there. Sue me for looking! I had pretended not to look or take an interest, but as a boob guy, it was tough.

When I saw the size in that black and white lettering, 34J, I wasn't surprised, but it made trying not to look at her or them even harder. So, I just pretended not to like her.

"All yours," I said without looking at her.

"Thanks," Roxy yawned.

Chris worked part-time at some big-time law firm in the mailroom. He had been there for over a year without the faint hint of being promoted or talking about getting a raise.

I told him to look for something else or show more interest in his job. But as they say, you can't lead a cow to water or some shit like that.

He always got ready early, even though he didn't need to be at work for another two hours. So, when I left, he was still downstairs.

I ventured out into the cold, busy New York air. I ran the two blocks to the gym. It was a good day, but since I was running late, I took it easy by doing some light weights, then more than my usual cardio. After being there for over an hour and a half, I decided to head back.

When I returned to the apartment, I heard them going at it in their room.

I sighed.

The walls in this place were paper-thin; the bed squeaked like it was about to break.

I could hear him moaning and groaning.

I hoped I didn't sound like that when I brought anyone home. I showered, quickly drying off and putting on my work clothes.

I worked for an advertising company. It wasn't a big deal, but it paid the bills, plus I liked it.

This lovely apartment in downtown New York wasn't cheap, so whatever they put in helped. Without them, I would be just scraping by and have to think of getting another job.

Pulling the tie-up to my neck. I looked in the mirror – the monkey suit was complete.

Coming out of the bathroom, I could hear that the rodeo in their room was over. As it usually was, it was sad. One night I timed them. From start to finish, it lasted just over three minutes.

I knew it had started some of their loud arguments, but that was none of my business.

I went downstairs to eat breakfast and heard the shower going.

Chris came down. His hair was still spiky.

"Hey," he said, looking away as usual.

He knew that I could hear.

"I should invest in soundproofing this place," I smiled.

To which he laughed.

"Yeah," he said, perking up.

He looked at the time and quickly ran out the door grabbing his bike. He usually biked it to work as it was close to our apartment.

I sat at the table, eating my breakfast.

Roxy came downstairs. She wore a business suit, a black dress that came down just above the knee, and a white top with a black blazer. Her hair was curly and down to her shoulders.

"Hi," she said.

"Hey," I replied.

We did not talk much, we had a few conversations, but it always had to do with Chris.

"I've got a few interviews today, so hopefully, one will pan out. Soon as I get enough, I will be out of your hair," Roxy said bitterly while taking some orange juice out of the fridge.

I took a deep breath.

"Look," I said. "You're not a bother, actually I don't mind having you guys here," I said honestly.

"Then what the fuck is it then?" Roxy said, slamming the fridge door closed. "Because I am getting tired of walking around here on eggshells!" she was infuriated.

There was that redhead anger I heard so much about.

"Nothing," I replied. "I'm just not a people person," I said with a shrug. I was honest. "The two of you walk around here all cheery, and that's just not me."

She looked at me, still furious.

"That's it?" Roxy said, throwing her hands. "What the fuck, kind of lame excuse is that?"

She was right. Of course, if someone had given me that excuse, I would say the same thing.

We lived in a large apartment, not large, but significant for this part of New York. And people, what people? Two of them. One of which was my best friend.

"Tell you what," I said, looking at her.

Those emerald green eyes stared right back at me. Daring me to say something stupid.

I smiled and took a deep breath.

I attempted to calm her down before she exploded or turned into some red-headed demon.

"Tonight, we will go out, all three of us and talk it out. Obviously, something's wrong, and I will admit that it's mostly me. Maybe Chris can come up with an answer, he knows me better than anybody," I said to which there were signs of the storm passing.

"Okay, but you better talk or... urghhh," Roxy said, slamming the orange juice bottle on the table. It burst open, spilling its contents everywhere.

She looked down at it.

"I'll get it," I said.

To which she grabbed a coat from the hallway and then stormed out. Slamming the door behind her.

I waited for a few seconds for my erection to fall. That was a turn-on for some reason. Maybe it was because, while Roxy was standing there, all I saw was her huge boobs swaying back and forth, her red hair tussling all over.

As I regained composure, I thought of other bullshit I could devise tonight. I couldn't tell them the truth: I was pretending to ignore Roxy because I secretly wanted her.

Chris had been my best friend for years. I couldn't do that to him.

"Fuck!" I screamed, looking at the time. Now I was late.

WHEN I GOT TO THE OFFICE, I only thought about Roxy and what I would tell her. I tried putting it out of my head, but it popped back in every time I tried.

"Martin?" my co-worker said.

"What?" I replied. I hated him with a passion.

You know that person at work that pisses you off just for the sake of pissing you off, but they don't realize they are doing it.

Yeah? Well, that's him.

"Did you see that show last night?" he asked across the hall.

"If I have to tell you one more time. I do not watch television," I said.

I didn't. There were two televisions in my apartment. The one in my room was not connected to the cable. I used it for my gaming system; the other was in their room.

Most television shows that are on television these days have turned many people into fat slobs that sit there and go into a coma for hours on end. Then they complained that they were overweight, well guess what. If they got off the couch and did other things, they wouldn't be.

"Oh yeah. Well, anyway, they have this show... Ouch!" he said as I threw a book at him. "Alright, fine." he surrendered.

Now, where was I? Oh yeah, Roxy. What could I do? She lived with me, right? Couldn't go the rest of however long we lived together just arguing? I could kick them both out. Chris and I had been through a lot. I am sure we will remain friends.

Damn it. Why couldn't Roxy be ugly or something?

The rest of the day dragged on.

We had a meeting in which I was shocked that an idea of mine would make it to the television. When we left the meeting, my boss patted me on the back.

"Congratulations," he said. "Go downstairs and start throwing your idea at them so they can get started on it," he ordered while walking away.

Great! Downstairs that's where I started in filming and development.

Do you know how long it takes to get a kid to sit still for thirty seconds to eat a bowl of cereal that tastes like a cardboard box?

No? Well, I do. And it was a very long time. Or a dog to chase its tail. I learned quickly that they don't like chasing their tail.

I was not too fond of every moment of filming. The director said this and then changed their mind to that.

"Martin, what brings you down here?" Adrian asked.

Talk of the stupid director.

"Hey, Adrian. I have this for you," I said, handing him the papers from the meeting.

I sat in his office, full of past pictures and ornaments of old advertisements for everything. You name it. It was up there.

"Who's the idiot that thought up this bunch of bullshit up?" he asked, tossing the folder on the table.

"This idiot," I replied with a smile.

"Seriously?" he asked, his jaw dropped.

"Yeah. Angel said to get started on it asap," I said.

I still got a few laughs from people when I told them that my boss's name was Angel.

"He did?" Adrian asked, picking up the folder. "So, what did you have in mind?" he said, looking at me.

We went into a long discussion about my idea, throwing ideas back and forth for what seemed like hours, which was more than half the day.

I left happy. Finally, we saw eye to eye.

It wouldn't be one of those cheesy or high-tech commercials, just a typical commercial.

Too bad I will only see it at work, but this was my job.

I left work satisfied and took the subway home. Forgetting all about what waited for me when I got there.

IT WAS ALREADY DARK when I opened the door.

The two of them sat all nice and prettied up.

'Fuck' I shouted in my head as I saw them stand up.

I cursed myself for bringing up going out.

All I wanted to do was lie down and play some games.

"You forgot," Chris said.

Damn him for knowing me.

"Yes and No. But I am not cancelling. Give me a few to change and stuff," I said, holding my finger up at Roxy, who was on the verge of transforming into the red devil.

I entered my room, grabbed some clothes, and went to the bathroom.

I could hear the she-demon downstairs, already exploding.

Taking a quick shower, I wondered where to go. Then I remembered there was this lovely rock cafe down the road. I had heard about it from someone.

It was within walking distance. Supposedly, it served excellent food and had couches where we could sit, talk, and listen to a local rock talent performing onstage.

Easy fifteen-minute walk, probably forty-five minutes inside, another fifteen minutes back, and voila. I smiled at myself for thinking about it.

"Okay, ready," I said as I headed downstairs.

"So where are we going?" Roxy asked.

There was a hint of sarcasm in there, but I ignored it.

"The new rock cafe down the street," I replied, to which both smiled.

We talked about going there many times.

"My treat," I said, opening the door.

"Phones," Chris said, pointing to the small table by the door.

Damn, his rule.

Anytime we went out, we left our phones at home. He hated it when phones went off in the middle of eating. I put my phone on the table. I saw theirs were already there.

It was a nice brisk walk down there. It took longer than frigging fifteen minutes, though, more like just over a half-hour.

But we talked more about Chris's job heading nowhere, and Roxy had a few interviews that went well. But all in all, it was a nice walk.

We entered the cafe, which was a hole in the wall. There were sofas and couches spread everywhere with tables in front of them. A small stage was set up in the corner, and a local band was setting up.

"Take a seat anywhere," said a man with black hair, slightly Gothic looking.

We sat in the corner and ordered some drinks and light finger food.

"So, talk," Roxy said.

'Crap! Already? We just got here,' I thought to myself. But it was the reason we were here. So, it was best to get right to it.

"Okay, so the reason that I gave you earlier is correct. Chris will tell you, I have never been a people person," I began to say.

"The worst is he actually got into arguments with his mother and still does," Chris said, nodding.

"But it doesn't mean that it's a reasonable excuse for shunning you like I have," I said.

"Correct," Chris chimed in.

"So, if we are going to live together, I will try, and I mean that. I will try hard not to ignore you or pretend you don't exist," I said to Roxy.

'Now, if you hid those huge fucking tits of yours, it would help a lot more,' I thought.

Roxy smiled, which, in the light, looked stunning. She had light makeup on. Her hair was wet and curly.

"Thank you, and I will try not to act all cheery," Roxy said, and we shook on it.

Roxy sat back on the couch and took off her jacket.

I looked away at the stage and then looked back at her.

'Really!' I said in my head loudly. *'Did she have to wear that?'* I thought to myself.

Roxy wore a black sheer mesh top with a black bra underneath. You could see the bra, top, or whatever it was underneath that almost nonexistent cover with a black skirt to mid-thigh and thigh-high black boots.

"Excuse me, that walk was a bit too long," I said, getting up.

Heading for the boy's room. I found a stall and slammed the door behind me.

'Holy Crap they were bigger than I thought. And those legs how I would love them wrapped around me.' I thought to myself.

"Calm down," I said to myself out loud. "You can do this."

That image was burned into my head. And there was nothing that could get it out. Wish I had my phone right now. I could call someone, anyone, for a pretend emergency right now.

There were plenty of bars around here I could hide in for the rest of the night. But I couldn't because of the stupid no-phone rule!

'Fuck!' I yelled at myself.

"Hey, Martin you alright in there?" Chris asked.

"Yeah, I am fine," I said back to him.

'Other than I want to fuck the living crap out of your girlfriend!' I thought but did not say it. I knew it would ruin our friendship.

"Okay just wondering, the band started, and the food is here," he said.

"Okay, I will be right there," I replied.

'Man up!' I said to myself, shaking it off. I stepped out of the bathroom.

"Sorry," I said to them as I sat back down, trying not to focus on her or them.

The lights dimmed as the band started playing.

They were alright, not good, but not terrible. I liked my rock a bit louder and heavier, but it was good.

We drank and began to talk, and with the lights dimmed, I could barely make out her outfit.

We talked, and I told them about my job and my idea that might make it to the couch potato box.

"Hey, sorry to bother you, but my friend wanted me to give you this," a woman said.

It was a refill of the drink I had ordered.

I looked over at the friend.

She was pretty but nowhere near my type, but hey, if it would get me away from these two for a while.

I looked over at Roxy and Chris. They both smiled.

"Go for it," Chris said.

Since I said it would be my treat, I left some money on the table. More than enough to cover the bill.

Roxy stared at the lady at the bar and then at the friend who delivered the note.

If looks could kill, they would be both dead.

I just took it as the queen bitch syndrome and walked away.

The rest of the night went well, and I found out the woman wasn't even close to being my type. She wasn't into working out. She loved reality shows and all that other crap.

The lights had turned back on for the next act, and even from here, I could make out Roxy's figure.

No way was I going back there even if I had to stay here and listen to reality television 101.

A few moments later, Roxy and Chris waved at me as they were leaving, and I waved back. I waited for about ten minutes, then said my goodbyes. I took her phone number and walked outside, throwing it in the nearest trash bin.

I walked the long way home, stopping at a bar on the way.

When I returned home, I slowly opened the door and crept upstairs to my room.

I lay in bed.

"Fuck I can't believe how big your tits are!" Chris moaned.

"No way not again!" I said to myself, pulling the pillow over my head.

"Come on fuck me!" there was Roxy.

'And here comes the squeaking,' I thought.

Right on schedule, the bed began its rhythmic squeakathon.

I turned over to look at the clock. 1:41 am, the bright red numbers glared back at me.

Roxy: "Come on fuck me harder."

Chris: "mm fuck."

Squeaky Squeaky.

Chris: "Damn I am getting close."

Squeaky Squeaky.

Roxy: "Don't stop keep going. "

Chris: "Fuck I can't."

Squeaky Squeaky.

Roxy: "Damn it!"

Chris: "I'm Sorry."

I looked back over at the time 1:43 am.

'Damn the boy needs help,' I thought.

I smiled, listened to them argue for a few minutes, and then dozed off.

Chapter Two: The Favor

The morning came; I woke up to do my usual routine.

Chris was again in the bathroom.

I swore again that one day I would put a lock on the door so he couldn't get in. Roxy came out of the bedroom with bed hair, a long black shirt, and pajama bottoms.

"Morning," she said.

"Morning," I replied.

We waited outside the bathroom.

"So how did it go last night?" Roxy asked.

"Went pretty well, left the cafe shortly after you did and grabbed a few drinks," I replied.

I didn't mention I left the woman there.

"Sounds good," Roxy said, rolling her eyes.

"Got her number," I said.

Hopefully, throwing off any scent she might have that I was interested in her. She looked at me sarcastically and then gave me the thumbs up.

"Tell him to hurry up. I will go in when you finish," Roxy said, turning around and returning to their room.

Chris came out, then walked past me without a word.

I got ready for the gym and headed downstairs. Chris was down there and was sitting at the table. He didn't look too good.

"What's wrong?" I asked. Pulling up a chair.

"You know what's wrong," he replied. "Don't act like you don't," he growled.

I took a deep sigh.

"Yeah, I know," I replied.

This was not a subject that guys talked to each other about. Either you got it, or you don't; if you don't, you should seek medical help.

"What can I do?" he asked.

I looked down at the table.

"See a doctor bro," I said. "That shit is more mental than physical half the time, it's not like you don't have the stamina I have seen you run."

The guy was like a marathon runner; he could run for hours.

Chris looked at the stairs, then motioned for the door. We walked outside. It was morning cold but not too cold. People walked by but paid no attention to us.

"I think she is too much for me," Chris said.

I looked at him like he was an alien or something.

"I never had this problem before. Remember Crystal?" Chris asked.

Do I?' I laughed as I thought that to myself. "Of course, the stick figure," I replied.

Crystal was five foot nine inches and weighed less than a hundred pounds. Or slightly more. She was a walking, talking stick figure. Anybody that saw her would agree.

"Yeah, her," Chris nodded with a smile. "I used to be able to go forever and Mary before her. But Roxy, from the very first time, it is like, pfft! Two minutes tops," he said, looking down at the floor.

I felt sorry for him, but what could I say? I never had that problem. Oh, wait.

"Cassandra," I said in a low voice.

"That was high school," he said.

"No! We met again shortly after college and well it happened a couple of times," I admitted.

Okay, I am human; shoot me! I felt sorry for the guy, and it didn't happen.

With Cassandra, it was weird between the two of us. I couldn't get it up with her very quickly, probably because the bitch took my virginity right after we graduated high school and ran. I never heard from her again until years later.

But still, a man's not a complete man if he can't get it up and stay up, so she laughed.

"Seriously?" Chris said with a smile.

"Yes, don't smile its creepy!" I said.

"So, what do I do? It's causing problems," Chris asked.

"Like I said seek help. It's probably in that noggin of yours," I said with a smile.

"Thanks," Chris said as he opened the door.

I ran to the gym, feeling better that I had helped him.

THE REST OF THE DAY went smoothly. Except for that, the debut for my commercial was tomorrow, and I had to be there. There were going to be some essential people from upstairs there as well.

I came home with lots of work to do.

Roxy sat at the table in the kitchen.

"Hey," I said.

She looked up with a smile.

"Hey," Roxy said. "I found a job!"

"Go you!" I replied. "Where at?"

"At that rock cafe. They gave me a card. I filled it out online. Sorry I used your computer," she was smiling.

"No problem," I replied.

"I start tomorrow!" Roxy giggled.

"Congratulations!" I smiled back. "Where's Chris?"

"He called and said he was working a double to get some overtime," she nodded.

'Good boy!' I thought. But I knew he probably went to see someone.

"Things are looking up," Roxy smiled and ran up the stairs.

I went back to my room and sat there, going over my notes. I fell asleep comfortably that night. I heard the door open and close. I looked up at the time. It was just past midnight.

It must have been Chris getting home late. Then I heard the familiar noise of the door across the hall open and close.

"WAKE UP!" I HEARD. Slowly I stirred. Roxy was leaning over me. "Wake up! Your late!" she said.

I looked over at the time. I was late.

"Why didn't my alarm go off?" I shouted.

She held my phone in her hand.

"You left it downstairs," Roxy said.

I ran into the bathroom. Thankfully Chris wasn't there today. Quickly getting dressed and ready in under twenty minutes.

I launched myself downstairs.

Roxy was wearing blue jeans and a grey crop top, with her car keys in her hand.

"I'll take you," she said.

She was the only one in the apartment that had a car.

It was New York, and only a few people drove. So, I didn't bother buying a car for myself.

"Thanks," I said.

There was no way I could get there on time by taking the subway.

"Taking Martin to work, Chris!" Roxy shouted up the stairs.

"He's home?" I asked as we left the apartment.

"Yeah, his boss told him to come in late because of the late shift he did last night," she said.

We got into her car, which was more of a small SUV than a car.

Roxy sped along the roads, ignoring many of the traffic signals. She reminded me of me when I used to drive.

"You look nervous," Roxy said over to me.

"That obvious huh?" I said my hands were shaking.

Today was big. I could get a raise and my own office if all went well.

"Crap my notes!" I shouted. I had left them at home.

"Want me to go back?" she asked, slowing down.

'And be really late?' I thought about it.

"No, I have all the ideas of what I have to say in my head." I said. "Keep going."

We reached the underground car park. Roxy parked in a spot.

"You look like shit!" Roxy said as she turned to look at me.

She was right. I was sweating, and my hands were shaking.

Roxy reached over to the glove box. Her chest rubbed against my thigh. Oh god, that didn't help matters. She grabbed some napkins.

"Here wipe that sweat away," she said, sitting back in her seat.

"Thanks," I said, wiping my brow and hands.

"How late are you?" Roxy asked.

I looked at the time.

"Thanks to you. I am ten minutes early," I sighed.

"See!" Roxy smiled, but then she looked down. "Oh," she said, staring at my pants.

I quickly tried to hide it.

"Sorry. I should go," I said, embarrassed.

"No, hold on," Roxy said. "So those videos I saw on your computer?" she asked.

"What Videos?" I said. Then I remembered that I was watching some porn before going to sleep the night before. I must not have exited out.

"You know the ones with the big chested women," she said.

"Yeah but... I really should go," I leaned for the door. Pushing it open.

"Really? You're going to walk in with that sticking out?" Roxy said, crossing her arms.

I came back in.

"Listen, I can help you," Roxy said. "You have helped me and Chris more than we can ever thank you, so think of it as a favor," she smiled.

"No, I couldn't," I said, shaking my head.

"Do you even know what I am talking about?" Roxy asked, staring at me.

I didn't, maybe a hand job at best if I was lucky.

"Get in the back!" Roxy ordered. Pulling her hair back in a ponytail.

"What? I can't Chris is my friend," I said, and I meant it.

"Get in the back!" Roxy shouted on the verge of she-devil's voice.

I quickly climbed in the back.

She quickly joined me. She reached to the side of my seat and pushed. The chair went back, and now she was kneeling between my legs.

"Chris doesn't have to know about this, and it is only a favor because you need this job, and if you go in there the way you are, you're likely to blow it. Understand?" Roxy said, looking up at me straight in the eyes.

All I could do was nod. The world was spinning. My best friend's girlfriend was about to do something sexual between my legs. If I was a good friend to Chris, I would open the door and get out right now. But it felt like I was paralyzed.

Roxy quickly grabbed my fly and pulled it down. Reaching inside, she grabbed my dick and then pulled it out. When she saw it, her eyes widened.

"Okay wow!" Roxy said with a pleasant surprise.

She started stroking it up and down with one hand while reclining the seat with the other now. She was directly above it.

"Didn't know you were working with this!" Roxy said pleasantly.

She pulled the tight crop top off.

"Now remember! Only a favor!" Roxy said.

I looked at her bra, it was purple lace, and it was losing the battle of holding a pair of the most enormous tits I had ever seen inside of it.

Roxy pushed my dick under the bra and between her gigantic tits. She grabbed the sides of the bra and quickly began bouncing her big tits up and down.

"Fuck that feels good," I said as Roxy held the side of her chest and rubbed them up and down against me.

The head of my dick never clearly made it higher than the peak of her cleavage.

She started going faster, bouncing her huge tits up and down on my dick.

"Damn you're lasting longer than Chris ever did when I tit fucked him," Roxy said as she pushed them together tighter.

"Fuck your good at this!" I said, feeling my dick between her tits.

I had been tit fucked before, but never with breasts this big.

"Come on, you got to cum now, or you will be late, Remember?" Roxy said.

Rubbing and twisting them around my dick.

"Fuck them. I want to stay here," I said.

Roxy smiled. Showing off her pearly white teeth.

"No, sit up look at your big dick between my tits," she said.

Roxy was smiling. She looked like she was enjoying this as much as I was. Which for me was a surprise as most women said they hated giving guys tit fucks as it did nothing for them.

As I looked, seeing my black dick being enveloped between her big milky white tits made me throb harder.

"Fuck, it is getting bigger!" Roxy said, rubbing them faster. She lowered her head and began to lick the head as it popped out, then she started sucking on the head.

"Fuck I'm cumming!" I said as I began to cum all over her chest.

"There! Feel better?" Roxy asked, pulling her tits off my dick and putting her shirt back on.

"Much!" I said my mind had cleared, and I wasn't sweating as much.

She grabbed a napkin and wiped the remaining cum off my dick.

"Thanks I..." I began to say.

"Just a favor. Never to be spoken of again or hinted at or repeated," Roxy winked at me.

Roxy climbed back into the driver's seat. I climbed out of the vehicle, closing the door behind me.

"Go kill 'em, champ!" Roxy said.

I nodded back at her as she sped off.

THE MEETING WENT PERFECTLY, as she said. I knocked it out of the park.

The commercial was a big hit with the execs, and they had decided to show it to the sponsors, who they said would gobble it up and put it on television soon. My boss shook my hand so much that I thought he would tear it off.

I had never felt so happy. I had gotten the raise that I wanted, as well as the office. No more annoying guy and no more thinking of getting another job.

I could pay my rent and theirs. We could move into a bigger apartment, one with two bathrooms. I smiled all the way home.

I opened the door and saw Roxy sitting at the table. She had a glum look on her face. She was still wearing the same shirt and jeans she had worn when she dropped me off. They must have called and told her they didn't need her to work.

I put down all my paperwork and headed for the table.

"Don't worry. There will be other jobs." I said, reaching out to hold her hand. She looked up at me with a lost look on her face; there was a note under her hand.

I reached for it.

Dear Roxy and Martin:

I don't know where to start, I wrote several letters yesterday and this morning and none sounded right. So, I will try to be like you, Martin, and just say it. I am leaving. No, I am not doing anything stupid like that. But I am going back to Florida.

You were right. When you both said, something was on my mind, keeping me from being me. The lack of interest at work, the lack of interest in our relationship. I went to seek help today, and in those few minutes of being there. I found out what had been holding me back for years.

It's this place, New York. It's not meant for me. The fast pace, the big lights, all of it. It has never felt like home. I know, Martin, when we decided to leave Florida together, we said that we were going because Florida was too slow and too behind the times. But I miss it. It suits me.

As soon as I started thinking about moving back, I began to feel better. Even now, writing this, I feel better inside. And I hope the two of you understand that this is the best for me, for us. I will always hold a place for the two of you.

If you ever forgive me for leaving like this instead of saying bye face to face. I hope you will contact me. I know our friendship Martin, and I know I will hear from you when you calm down. And I hope the same for you, Roxy, but I understand if I never hear from you again.

As one last favor friend to friend, Martin, will you take care of her? I know you will.

Always your friend

Chris.

That night we sat there, taking turns reading the letter. Trying to find something that would change. That would tell us our friend would come back.

Chapter Three: The Reaction

It has been just over six months now since Chris walked out. I want to say it had been for the best and that we have worked things out. But that would be a lie.

Chris moved back to Florida. At first, he moved back in with his mom for a while, but then he found a new girlfriend and moved out with her.

Roxy, his ex-girlfriend, moved out of the apartment two weeks after Chris had left. I saw her now and then. She still works at the rock place we had all gone out to for dinner the night before he left.

It seems like only yesterday we were all together in this apartment. But that's how memories are, right?

We can remember things that happened years ago, just as vivid and intense as if they happened just moments ago.

I blame myself a lot for Chris leaving. If I hadn't talked to him about setting himself straight, maybe he would have stayed, and our friendship wouldn't have fallen apart. But that's a lot of maybes.

Now I must deal with the present.

My job at the firm is a lot better. So much that I could afford to move out, I could finally afford a better apartment for myself.

I knew I must do a few things before I left. One of which was to return some of Roxy's things.

When she left, she forgot a lot of stuff. Some were Chris's, but I could ship those down to him.

I could leave a note at her workplace to come by and pick them up. I know she still has the key; she comes by when she knows I am not home. She usually picks up any mail that hasn't been forwarded to her new address.

But that's about it.

No, it is better to do something like this in person. Leaving a note would be as bad as Chris leaving her, with just a note for a goodbye.

I picked up the large bag holding the two boxes and walked out. It was not that long of a walk to Roxy's workplace. She should be working. It's Friday night.

Slowly I walked down the streets of New York, thinking of things I could say, trying to play out the conversation in my head. Before I knew it, I was outside of her workplace. I sighed and shook my head of any negative thoughts about how this would go down.

I walked inside. The girl by the door took my coat and pointed me to a chair or sofa that wasn't taken. I pointed to a chair and table by the window and walked towards it. I scanned the area, no sign of her yet. I saw the band making their final test of their equipment.

Hearing local rock talent is quite amusing. You can see their fears, their thoughts, and hopes in their eyes.

I saw Roxy coming out of the kitchen area. She had not spotted me yet. Maybe I could get out before she noticed me. I pushed that thought out of my head and stayed where I was.

Roxy looked my way, and she had the deer in headlights look for a second. I feared she would return to the kitchen and have someone else wait on me. But then she began to walk towards me.

"Hey," I said as she sat in the chair opposite me.

"Hey," Roxy replied.

Roxy's long red hair was still as radiant as the first day I saw her. Her eyes were not as bright. She was not smiling.

"I came to drop off a few things that you had left," I said, breaking the silence.

I pushed the bag over to her, to which she glanced inside and smiled.

"Oh, thanks; I meant to come by and get them, but..." Roxy paused, not knowing what to say.

"Yeah, I know," I nodded. "But I didn't want to just leave them behind," I began to say before realizing what I was saying.

"You're moving?" Roxy asked with a stunned look on her face.

"Yeah, I'm getting a bigger place closer to my job. It's in Manhattan," I said, trying not to sound like a total asshole.

"Ah making that big money now huh?" Roxy said with a smile.

"You can say that," I replied.

We both looked at the band as they introduced themselves to the crowd.

"Well, I wish you luck," Roxy said as she began to stand.

"Hope we can stay in touch," I said.

But I knew just like everyone knows. No one stays in touch. Slowly the communication slows, and then it just stops.

"Yeah of course," Roxy said with a smile, and her head cocked to the side.

She began to turn away.

"Wait," I said, shaking my head.

She looked back.

"Not like this okay?" I said, pointing to the chair.

Roxy takes a sigh and then sits back down.

"Not going to do this again. I have done it way too many times," I said, shaking my head.

"I know, so have I," Roxy said, sitting back in her chair and crossing her arms under her massive chest.

Her black shirt did nothing to hide them.

We sat in silence for what seemed like an eternity.

"I am not keeping you from working, am I?" I asked, finally.

"No, I just clocked out. I am just waiting for Charlie to get off so he can drive me home," Roxy said, nodding toward the guy working the soundboard by the stage. "I sold my car."

"Ah. I Thought you lived a few blocks from here?" I asked, knowing the answer already.

Roxy lives just a few blocks away. But it was in a bad neighborhood. It wasn't the worst but not the type you wanted to be walking around alone, especially after dark.

"Yeah," Roxy hesitated. "You want to walk with me?" she asked.

I was surprised. It wasn't what I expected.

"Sure," I said.

I had grown accustomed to the streets of New York.

I always thought of it like this; every state has natural disasters. Florida has hurricanes, California has earthquakes, and New York has high crime rates. Once you thought of it like that, it was almost comforting.

We began to walk first in silence. Then after a few minutes, the conversation picked up. Roxy told me about living with her roommate, who she hated, but the rent was cheap.

Roxy stated that she didn't like the roommate because, in Roxy's mind, the roommate was almost like a low-budget prostitute, constantly having different guys every night. These guys would also buy the roommate stuff that she wanted.

I talked about my job. I also told her there was talk of me being promoted again.

I had already seen the two men approaching us from behind and knew that one of them had a gun. But I had not made any sign to her.

Roxy gave me a slight nudge letting me know she had acknowledged them.

We kept talking as I rounded the upcoming corner. I turned around very sharply as they came about. I quickly turned.

"Hi!" I said, grabbing the one closest to me.

I shoved him into the wall. The other pulled out the gun.

"Your friend here, should talk a bit quieter," I launched myself at him shoving the gun out of his hand. "It's not loaded," I said to him.

"But this is," the other one had quickly grabbed Roxy holding a knife to her.

But she grabbed his wrist. She twisted it hard. Like most women in violent cities. Roxy had taken self-defense classes.

He let the knife go, and then they both ran away.

I stood there shaking; my heart was beating a mile a minute. Roxy did not look any better.

Kicking the gun down a sewer, I grabbed her hand and ran for it.

"I'm sorry. I shouldn't have done that!" I said as we reached a bar that was still open.

Roxy nodded and walked inside. We sat down in one of the corners. I could see she was visibly shaken. It had become an instinct.

Every time I had been mugged, I always fought it. I had gotten stabbed once and shot at twice. But I still did it.

"Chris told me about the first time," she said.

I attempted a half-smile.

"I shouldn't have done that with you present. It was stupid," I shook my head.

The waitress came by. We ordered two drinks mainly to take the edge off.

"That was my first," Roxy said, still shaking.

"He told you about our first then?" I asked.

She nodded.

I still remember it as if it happened recently.

Chris and I had been in New York a week before we were mugged at gunpoint. We gave up all our money and whatever else we had of value.

I never forgot that feeling of being helpless and lost after it had happened. That feeling stayed with me for weeks. I was constantly looking over my shoulder for the next attack. Then one day, I swore I would rather die than feel like that again.

I looked up at her.

"Yeah, it still bugs me to this day," I said.

"I understand," Roxy said with a smile. "Next time, give me a heads up?"

We both laughed.

The drinks came, and we both began to relax a little.

"So how is he doing?" Roxy asked, putting her beer down.

I knew this was coming.

"Good," I said, trying not to answer fully. "Moved out of his mom's," I added.

"Found a girl then, huh?" she asked.

She knew Chris very well. He would never live on his own.

I just looked up at her.

"Take that as a yes," Roxy half-smiled. "Good for him," she said, looking up at one of the many televisions that were showing sports.

"Well let's get you home," I said, taking out my phone.

I called the local police station.

"Hi. I just heard some shots fired down the block, and heard screeching tires," I said.

Roxy smiled as I put on a different voice. I tried to sound like Chris, who always did this when he wanted to go somewhere. I gave the address to a random street corner.

They never actually investigated it. They would send a patrol car around the block. If they spotted something worth exploring, then more would show up.

We sat talking about other things that came up, particularly her not getting enough hours at work to pay her half of the rent. She also told me about a guy she met who stood her up after finding out she didn't give blow jobs. It was one of her things. I never asked why or cared.

Soon we saw the patrol car make its way past the bar.

"That's our cue," Roxy said as we hurried out.

As if most people in the bar heard us, many left the money on the table and hurried out the door. For at least four blocks, any thieves or muggers would have seen the car and cleared out for at least a half-hour or more.

"We can't get to my place, without going back," Roxy said, looking back at the way we came.

The two men had seen where we were heading and were probably waiting for payback with friends.

"My place?" I asked.

She nodded.

We hurriedly walked the other way towards my place, which was a long walk but much safer.

As we approached the door, she reached into her pocket and took out the keys.

"Instinct," Roxy said, smiling as she opened the door.

Walking in, she saw most of the boxes lining the floor.

"Sorry for the mess," I said as she stepped over the boxes.

"You said you were moving." Roxy shrugged as she went into the kitchen. Her phone rang.

"Yeah, I am okay." Roxy turned away from me as she headed upstairs. "Staying at a friend's house until the morning," I heard her say before the door closed.

It felt good having her here. I turned the kitchen light off and then went into my room. I heard her walking around. Then the shower turned on shortly after it turned off. There was a knock on my bedroom door.

"It's open," I said.

She opened it, turning on the light. I sat up in bed.

"What's up?" I asked.

Roxy was standing in the doorway. With one of my long shirts on, I could tell she had nothing under that.

"Is it alright if Charlie picks me up in the morning?" Roxy asked. "It will be early, and I don't want to wake you," she said.

"Of course, I usually wake up early anyway," I said, trying not to think of what was under that shirt.

"Thanks," Roxy said as she closed the door.

I could lie and say I didn't think about her for the rest of the night, but I won't. The truth is, I did not sleep much. Knowing she was alone and only a few feet away from me made me think of many things.

When I heard the front door close, I knew she was gone, and it was only then I got some sleep. Not a lot, though.

WORK WAS THE USUAL drag. Even though I was moving up the corporate ladder, as they would say, it was still a drag. Full of people that I hated, others I tolerated, and only a few that I got along with.

As I looked over some sketches for the next cycle of soda ads, my phone vibrated in my pocket. I picked it up, thinking it was one of my co-workers asking where we were going for lunch. I was surprised to see a text message from Roxy.

'*What do you think?*' it said.

I scrolled down to the picture. I almost fell out of my chair.

Roxy was wearing a black and red mini dress, with the chest cut out just enough to show her ample cleavage. To say it was form-fitting was an understatement.

'*Wow, very nice,*' was the only reply that would not make me sound too interested.

'*Going out clubbing tonight with Charlie and a few friends. First time I have been out in a long time. Thought I would buy something new,*' was her reply.

'*Well, that should turn a few heads,*' I replied.

I looked over the picture again.

'*Thanks. You should come,*' Roxy sent back.

I hated clubbing more than I hated watching television.

'*Nah. You guys should go and have fun,*' I replied.

I wouldn't make up a lie to get out of it.

'You owe me for last night. You're coming. Be ready by ten!' Roxy said Before I could reply and try and get out of it. *"End of conversation!"* she sent.

I put the phone down.

How could I argue? I did owe her for putting her in that situation and many other things. I sighed and thought of things I could wear.

Did I mention I hated clubs?

The rest of the day went by fast after that. I kept thinking about things for the night, like what to wear? Who was going? How long did I have to go?

I really didn't want to go, but the chance to see Roxy in that dress in person might make it worth it.

Chapter Four: The Act

It was moments to ten when I finally decided on a black shirt that was very tight.

I wasn't one of those guys putting those shirts on and had their stomachs out. I looked good excellent in tight shirts. I also choose black jeans, with black sneakers.

Looking in the mirror one more time. I thought I looked damn good.

There was a knock on the door. Looking over at the time. I realized I had spent more time getting dressed than any guy should.

When I looked over at my bed, there were clothes everywhere. I didn't particularly appreciate how they looked spread all over it. I quickly scooped them up in both hands, opened the walk-in closet, and threw them in.

I looked around to ensure there was no other sign that I had been a nervous wreck for the past four hours. Satisfied, I ran downstairs.

"Hey, was beginning to think you were not going to answer," Roxy said.

She was wearing a mini dress. The skirt part stopped just about mid-thigh, and the red stripe ran down both sides of the black dress. She was wearing a black blazer over the top, but I knew a keyhole-shaped opening was right at chest level.

Part of me wished she would keep that blazer on all night; another wanted to see what was under it.

"Nah was just trying to get a few more kills in on the game," I said, lying through my teeth as I locked the door.

"Ah!" Roxy said as she walked towards a green sports car. "Charlie is waiting for us."

"Fun," I said sarcastically as I walked towards the car.

Roxy opened the door and got into the back seat. I glanced at her thighs as she pulled the passenger seat back. Then I got into the front.

"Hey what's up?" Charlie said from the driver's seat.

I recognized him from her workplace. Small frame, brown hair, bright blonde highlights. She must have a thing for blonde guys, I thought to myself.

"Hey," I replied as we pulled away.

Another guy was in the back seat, but I didn't get his name over the roaring engine.

I had no idea why Charlie was trying to show off. He would speed up every chance he got, but we would have to come to a complete stop at every intersection.

Finally, we got to the club. We stepped out. Charlie had them valet park his precious gas guzzler.

I noticed that Charlie had begun talking to the guy from the back seat as we walked in. They both laughed and giggled.

"Relax," Roxy said from beside me as we entered the club.

"I am," I replied.

No, I wasn't. I had just stepped inside the club, and I was already getting stares from the bouncer and other guys inside the club.

We all know the looks. Who is he? and why is he wearing that? Does he think he is tough or something? Yeah, those stares.

We found a place to sit with a good dance floor view. I had to admit it was a nice club.

The bar was lit with bright neon colors. The dance floor was enormous; the upstairs level had a view of everything. The music was loud, but it was supposed to be. No club wanted you to sit and talk all night. They wanted you to drink and dance.

Charlie and the other guy joined us shortly. Then two other ladies joined us. I barely heard the conversation, but they were all friends from the same workplace. When they introduced me, I lightly shook their hands and smiled.

"Do you dance?" one of the ladies asked.

I knew this question was coming, so I had practiced the reply countless times.

"He is a great dancer!" Roxy shouted back before I could reply.

"Great!" the lady replied, taking my hand before I could interject.

I shot Roxy a killer stare as we walked toward the dance floor. She was half right. I was good at dancing, not great, but I could hold my own.

Before long, I was getting into the groove on the floor and having a great time. The music was as I liked: loud with heavy beats and some mixes.

We began to walk back to our spot as we had gotten thirsty. Roxy and Charlie were gone, and so was the other guy. I reminded myself that I would get his name when he came back.

The lady I danced with was Corrine. She had a nice ass, which had been rubbing up on me for the last half hour. Long black hair and a cute face. Her husband was working a night shift, so she took this time to enjoy herself.

I looked over at the dance floor and saw Charlie and Roxy dancing. I had never seen her dance before, and I was genuinely amazed. I was staring hard. She knew how to work her body.

"Wow!" the other lady said.

Her name was Yessica. She was Latin and had no boyfriend or husband. But from the attitude I heard earlier, it was no wonder she was single. The world revolved around her, and she wanted everyone to know it.

"White girl has some moves!" Yessica said.

"Can say that again?" Corrine said.

I was glad I wasn't the only one staring. No wonder Chris had a hard time in the bedroom. I began to think.

"Poor Charlie," I said.

The two women looked at me.

"Why?" Corrine asked.

"Looks like he bit off more than he can chew," I said as I saw Roxy grinding her firm ass against him.

They both still looked at me, puzzled.

"What?" I asked.

"You do know Charlie is gay, right?" Yessica said. She was more telling me than she was asking me.

I looked over at Corrine. Who nodded back at me.

"Could have fooled me," I said.

The guy had moves of his own.

Glad my gaydar didn't work because I would have sworn from the looks and the way he was dancing he was as straight as an arrow.

"Paul is his boyfriend or husband. However, you want to think of it," Yessica said, frowning.

A guy approached her and asked her to dance, and she walked away.

"Don't mind her," Corrine said. "She acts tough, but she is all talk," she laughed.

Charlie and Roxy came back to the table.

"Here you guys are. We were looking for you out there," Charlie said.

"Come on," Roxy said as her song came on.

I recognized it right away. Roxy played the hell out of it daily when she lived with me.

Roxy grabbed my hand and pulled me to the dance floor. She took her blazer off and threw it at Charlie. I instantly stole a glance at her deep cleavage.

"Try to keep up!" Roxy smiled back at me.

"Do I look like Charlie?" I laughed.

We began to dance close, with her facing me. I tried not to focus on her chest, but it was hard.

Roxy lifted one leg and wrapped it around me, and fell backward. I reached forward, grabbed her neck lightly, and pulled her back up. She laughed as she slowly spun around, grinding back on me. I grabbed her waist as she bent over.

Damn, this was a nice view, but I quickly kept my concentration and bumped her forward with my hips. She smiled and walked away. Shaking her ass with her hands on her hips.

She ran her fingers through her hair, biting her lip, motioning for me to come closer to her. She wrapped both arms around my head and neck as I got closer, swinging her hips back and forth. She slowly turned, facing away from me, her ass rubbing close to my crotch.

I suddenly felt another pair of hands around my waist and another body close to mine.

Slightly turning my head backward, I saw Corrine had joined us.

The two women danced with me for over an hour. I felt sandwiched between them, but I was not complaining.

After the DJ announced it would be the last song before he would do a set of slow songs, we stopped and walked back to the table. I took the chance to go to the bathroom.

I opened one of the stalls looking in the mirror. My shirt was soaked, as well as my face. I had done my best to keep up with both, and it showed. I began washing my face when I heard some other guys enter the bathroom.

"Did you see that guy with those two white girls?" one of them asked.

I smiled unless more than one guy was dancing with two women; they were talking about me.

"Yeah, the red head with the rack had some moves. Poor guy was lost!" the other said.

I was sure as hell was not lost. Would like to see them keep up.

"That other one was all ass. I would like to get behind that for sure," the first one said.

I shook my head. Throwing some paper towels into the trash and flushing the toilet to get their attention. I opened the stall and stepped out.

The both of them looked at me as they were washing their hands. I smiled and shook my head, then walked out of the bathroom. I am sure they said more after I left.

As I walked over to our table, I noticed a few guys by our table talking to Roxy and Corrine. I smiled but slowly walked over until I realized these people worked for the club.

"Well, think about the offer and get back to us," one of the men said as I got close. "Hey," he said as I walked by him. "If you can get him to join also that would be awesome!" he said, pushing two thumbs up.

Roxy nodded.

"What was that about?" I asked, looking around for the others.

"Tell you on the way," Roxy said as we left the club.

We got into Corrine's car and drove over to a diner.

They told me what the men had asked them. They both got job offers to work at the club as dancers.

We spotted the others in a corner booth as we entered the diner.

"You guys should definitely take the offer," I said as we sat down.

"Take what offer?" Charlie asked.

Soon the conversation was in full swing. But it started to die down as quickly as Yessica showed up.

"What's going on, fools?" she said, sitting down.

She injected herself into the conversation. But had nothing positive to say at all.

"You're a good dancer, but you don't have any good clothes to wear. Except for that one," she said, pointing to the one Roxy was wearing. "And that took you two paychecks to get!"

Roxy's smile went away. Yessica looked over at Corrine.

"You're lucky your man let you out tonight. I am sure he wouldn't let you out every weekend to dance," she said, taking some of Charlie's fries.

This made everyone silent.

"What? Can't handle honesty?" Yessica said, shrugging.

"Honesty is one thing. Being unrealistic is another," I said.

To which Roxy hit me with her elbow. It took me one night to notice no one stood up to this bitch. Yessica looked at me with a stare that could kill.

"The reason you don't want them to take the job is that they would rain on your spotlight," I began to say. "Only one guy came up to you tonight. I guess that pissed you off since Roxy and Corrine got most of the attention without even trying. Now you want to tear them down to make yourself feel better!"

To which others smirked.

Yessica stood up. "I don't have to take this!" she said, walking out.

"You should not have done that," Corrine said.

"She had it coming," Charlie said, to which they agreed.

"I better go," Corrine said.

She was visibly displeased at the whole situation.

Charlie and his boyfriend looked like they wanted to go as well.

"We can get a cab," I said, not trying to keep them away from whatever they wanted to do.

As if I had rung the lunch bell, they took off. Roxy looked at me.

"What?" I asked.

"You know what!" Roxy said, shaking her head.

I waved the waitress over and paid the bill.

"Sometimes you have to put a filter on that brain of yours," Roxy said as we began to walk out of the diner.

"Did I tell a lie?" I asked.

"No, you didn't, but some people can't handle the truth. Well, the blatant truth," she said as we waited outside.

The waitress had called a cab for us.

"This is going to be a fun week," Roxy said, shaking her head. She was visibly cold.

"Here," I said, taking off my jacket and wrapping it around her.

"Thanks," Roxy said. "But you will be cold too," she pulled me close and wrapped her arms around me, placing her head on my chest. "Promise me you will be nice to her next time. I do have to live with her."

"Well maybe it will be the last time I will see her," I smiled.

We both laughed as the cab pulled in. I opened the door for Roxy and climbed in after her.

"Well, you can stay in your old room tonight. It will give her time to calm down," I said as we settled in the back of the cab.

Roxy nodded that it was just as cold inside as it was outside. I told the driver where to go and paid half the fare upfront as it was right.

I opened the door to the apartment and waved the cab driver goodbye. It was nice of him to watch us get into the apartment, but I am sure he thought it was only fitting with the big tip I gave him.

Roxy quickly walked over to the heating unit and dialed it up.

"Sheesh, it's like a morgue in here!" Roxy said, shivering.

She went to the fridge and poured herself a drink.

"You just don't like the cold," I said as we sat in the small kitchen.

Roxy got up, took the jacket off, and her petite blazer revealed the keyhole cut in her dress. I had seen it most of the night, but now in the light, her cleavage was too much.

"Well, I guess I will call it a night," I said, pretending to yawn and stretch.

Roxy slammed the cup down on the table.

"How do you do that!" Roxy said out loud.

"What?" I asked, sitting back down.

Something told me the redhead was going to explode again.

"You can tell people off, and say you're just being honest. But you can't sit here with me and be honest with yourself!" Roxy said, staring right at me.

I tried my best to look at her, but I couldn't. Even though she was no longer my friend's girl, there was just no way I could look at her. Knowing I was the one that had caused their separation.

"I can but..." I began to say.

"Don't even. You're just going to bend the truth just enough to make me feel good," Roxy said, shaking her head.

Roxy grabbed a chair and pulled it close, so we were face to face.

"You want honesty?" Roxy said, looking me straight in the eyes. "You know the real reason why I left?"

She shook her head and smiled.

"I fought myself to feel angry, upset, or even depressed about Chris leaving. I even tried to feel guilty for what I did with you. But I couldn't," Roxy said, sitting back in her chair and throwing her hands up. "I felt happy it was over. Chris and I never really clicked. Sure, we had fun. But never really clicked, and as far as what I did with you."

Roxy was leaning forward. Staring me dead in the eye.

"I was going to tell him. I was going to tell him what I did and that I have wanted to do that and more since I met you," shaking her head. "There. There is your honesty!"

She stood up, looking down at me.

"At least one of us can be honest with ourselves," Roxy said, walking out of the kitchen.

I don't know what came over me, but I quickly stood up, grabbed her hand, turned her around, and kissed her. She began to kiss me back as we slammed into the kitchen wall.

"About time!" Roxy said as we parted.

"Shut up," I smiled as we began to kiss again.

With her back against the wall, she lifted her leg and wrapped it around me. I quickly grabbed it with one hand and stroked her thigh under the skirt. She began to moan softly as I bit her neck and kissed her. Her leg dropped as I rubbed and squeezed her ass.

"They are up here," Roxy said, grabbing my hand and putting it on her chest.

I have big hands, but they seemed small compared to her massive chest. I quickly scooped her up.

Both her legs wrapped around me as I carried her upstairs. Lightly kicking my bedroom door open. I planted her down on the bed.

"Such force!" Roxy said, looking up at me as I climbed over her. "I like it!" she said, smiling.

I smiled back and kissed down her body, lightly lifting her skirt.

"Zipper!" Roxy said before I began to rip it off her.

I reached up and pulled the zipper down as the outfit peeled off her.

Revealing a strapless black bra and matching thong.

"Damn!" I said, looking at her lovely body.

Her stomach was nice and tight; her long thighs went down to beautiful legs and feet. But her chest breathed up and down with those huge breasts heaving with it.

I laid down between her legs, pushing her legs apart. Slowly I slid a finger into her. She moaned as she felt my breath on her. I pushed my tongue inside her joining my finger, working it all around.

Roxy's moans got louder. Sliding another finger into her drove the cries louder as her body began to move and grind down on my tongue and face.

I was getting turned on by her noises, so I kept going deeper and faster, working on her clit with my tongue.

This began to drive her crazy as her hands grabbed the sheets and pulled on them. I worked her warm pussy more with my tongue.

Her body arched as an orgasm erupted inside her. She began to push her boobs together, sucking on the nipples.

"Don't stop!" Roxy screamed as I continued.

I gripped her hips with my arms.

"Oh my god! Right there!" Roxy said as she grabbed my head with both hands pushing my head into her.

I had no intention of stopping.

"Fuck!" Roxy squealed as her body arched again for the second time. "Okay! Enough! Enough!" she said, pushing me back with her feet.

"Fuck me now!" she ordered.

I took off my shirt and jeans in a quick second. My rock-hard dick poked through my boxers.

"Mm... mm..." she moaned, looking at it.

I pulled them off. I slid back between her legs. She looked at me as she sucked on a nipple again with teasing eyes.

"Put it in me big boy!" Roxy smiled.

I nodded as I put my dick at her entrance and slowly moved forward. Her mouth instantly went into an O as I slid inch by inch into her.

"Okay stop right there!" she said.

I was barely halfway into her. But I remembered what she had worked with before and slowly started going back and forth, working more into her.

"Fuck that feels good!" I said.

I wasn't lying, either. Roxy's pussy was hot and tight. Tighter than most of the women I had ever been with.

I leaned back, grabbing her legs and splitting them wide apart as I slowly rocked back and forth into her. Watching my black dick go in and out of her made me harder.

"Like what you see!" Roxy said, breathing heavily.

I nodded as I kept looking. My dick was sliding in and out of her. Getting coated with her wetness. She was taking more of me, and she loved it.

"Go faster!" Roxy said as she held both of her tits up to her mouth.

"Fuck yeah suck on them big tits!" I said, looking at her.

I pushed forward, holding myself over her body. With my arms on each side of her, looking down at her as she looked up at me.

Roxy kept her legs wide as I fucked her deeper; she took me in. The sound of my balls slapping against her filled the room.

"Fuck yeah take it all!" I said, pushing deeper with each thrust.

She pulled me down on top of her wrapping her legs around my waist. I kept thrusting up in her back and forth. The poor bed squeaked and slid back and forth under us.

"You're so fucking deep!" Roxy said into my ears.

Her legs locked tighter behind me as she squeezed them closer, pushing me deeper into her. Her ankles were digging into my lower back. I felt her body quiver again, and her mouth made an inaudible scream. She was cumming again.

I wrapped my arms under her, then up, grabbing her shoulders. I began pulling them down with each upthrust.

Her eyes popped open.

I pushed myself up off her, breaking free of her leg lock on me. I wanted to fuck her harder than anyone ever had or would. Grabbing both legs. I put them together and pushed them forward over her head so they nearly touched the backboard.

"Oh god!" Roxy screamed as I fucked down onto her.

She held her legs looking up at me with tears in her eyes.

"Fuck me! fuck me!" Roxy yelled loudly. "Fucking use me!"

She was now soaking the bed. Every time she came. I fucked down harder and harder.

I was on the verge of cumming. But I wanted to fuck her so much more.

"'I'm Cumming!" I said, finally giving in.

She let her legs go.

"Cum on my tits!" she said.

I quickly pulled out and straddled her chest as I came. The first blast shot her straight in the face. The others landed on her tits as she pushed them together. When I finished, she began to lick her tits clean.

I fell to the side of her, breathing heavily. She turned and leaned on me, giving me a big kiss.

"I take that as a compliment," I smiled.

"You better!" Roxy slapped me lightly on the shoulder. She laid her head on my chest. "I can't feel my lower body."

She grabbed my arm and rolled over on her side. She held my hand on one of her enormous tits. We fell asleep like that.

THE MORNING CAME QUICKLY. I woke up on my back. Roxy was lying on her stomach, her red hair all over the place. I smiled, remembering what happened that night. Feeling me stirring, she opened her eyes.

"Morning," Roxy said.

"Morning," I said as I began to get up.

"Where are you going?" she asked.

"The gym. I am kind of late," I smiled.

Roxy shook her head. Pulling me back to bed. We kissed deeply, and her hands wandered down my chest. She wrapped her hand around my hardening dick.

"Morning wood," Roxy said. "I shouldn't waste it."

She kissed my chest, slowly working her way down. Her head disappeared under the covers. Then I felt her mouth wrap around my dick. I couldn't believe she was going to do this.

Roxy had never done this with Chris. I heard him complain nearly daily about it.

The covers began to go up and down right where her head was.

"Fuck that feels good!" I said as she began to go faster.

She was not the best I ever had, but the feeling of her doing it was more than the actual act.

She stopped and came up.

"I'm sorry," Roxy said, shaking her head. "I can't, I want to..." she began to speak.

"It's okay," I said, smiling at her.

She shook her head. Then told me why she didn't like doing it.

She first tried it just after high school with a college man. He did not like how she was doing it, so he grabbed the back of her head. Basically, skull fucked her until he came down her throat. He didn't allow her to catch a breath or anything and held her head down while he came. Then left her the very next day.

"First that would never happen to you again," I said, holding her close. "Second you don't have to do anything you don't want to."

Roxy smiled and nodded.

"But there is something I like to do, and I am very good at!" Roxy said, sliding herself out of bed.

Roxy left the room but patted the end of the bed before leaving.

I sat at the end of the bed. As Roxy returned, she had some baby oil lotion in her hands and rubbed it into her tits. Instantly my dick hardened to a fully upright position.

She sat on her knees between my legs, grabbing both tits and wrapping them around my dick. Instantly it felt great. She began bouncing them up and down.

"How does that feel?" Roxy asked as she bounced them faster.

Words did not escape my mouth. I could barely keep myself upright. Roxy's big oily boobs bounced around my dick and slapped heavily on my thighs. Even when I looked down between her huge oily tits, I could barely see the head of my dick barely reaching the top.

"You like your dick being buried between my big fucking boobs. Don't you?" Roxy said. Teasing me.

"Fuck yeah!" I replied.

Roxy began to bounce them harder. Up and down over and over. Her arms wrapped around them, making them tighter.

"Oh, fuck I am going to cum!" I couldn't believe it.

I tried to hold it back, but it was already too late. Roxy held them both tight around me as I shot up through them.

"Well, I take that as you being satisfied?" Roxy laughed.

I nodded my head as we lay back on the bed. There was a loud thump downstairs. We both looked at each other.

I quickly put some clothes on and headed down. I felt a sharp pain across my face as I turned the corner. I stumbled backward.

"Hi Chris," I said, shaking the feeling off.

Chris stood in the doorway to the kitchen, his fist clenched. He came at me again, but I grabbed him and planted him face-first into the wall this time. Holding him there.

"First one was a freebie!" I said, letting him go. "You try it again and I will hurt you I promise!"

He looked back at me. Chris was an intelligent person even when anger took over him. He knew I was a better fighter than he was.

"How?" Chris said, shaking his head.

Roxy came down the stairs as she saw Chris; she shook her head.

"You don't get to ask how!" Roxy said, walking straight past me. "How, why and all the other questions you want to ask left when you walked out that door!" she said, pointing to the door.

Chris nodded. "I understand you; I understand why you did this to me!" he said to her.

"But you!" Chris said, pointing to me. "We were friends, brothers even! And you slept with her the moment I was gone!" he shouted.

I could not look him in the face. He was right.

"If the roles were reversed you would whoop my ass all over this apartment. And I would let you. Because brothers don't do that!" he said as he walked out the door.

I fell backward on the stairs sitting down. Chris was right. If the roles were reversed, I would be pissed.

"His wrong, you know," Roxy said, sitting beside me. I looked up at her. "A brother would not walk out and leave without a word. He stopped being your friend and brother the moment he started thinking about himself," she said, holding her hand out.

I slowly stood up.

"Doesn't make it feel right," I told her.

"I know," Roxy said as she hugged me. "I know."

Chapter Five: The Aftermath

Chris sat on the floor just outside the door of his new job. He flicked the cigarette he had just finished into the far corner of the parking lot, took a deep breath, and returned inside. The mailroom was as busy as he had left it.

"Finally, back from your break, huh?" His boss shouted at him when he came back inside; Chris hated him. He wanted to punch the small fat man in the face every day.

"Nope, just came in to make sure you had not eaten everybody," Chris whispered.

"What was that wise ass?" the boss said.

Chris nearly repeated it, but he decided not to. Martin had put his reputation on the line to get Chris this job, and Chris needed it to pay his bills.

"Nothing," Chris muttered.

"Good. Now take load twenty, up to the legal department," he said, pointing to one of the large carts.

"What?" Chris said.

Chris looked at the large cart with the number twenty written on the side. The cart was filled with mail bags, ranging from small to extra-large.

"My time is up at five. It will take me until seven to get through all that," Chris said.

"Last time I checked you told me you needed the extra hours?" the boss said. "Anybody needs..." he began to speak to the rest of the room.

"I'll do it," Chris muttered.

Chris grabbed the cart and then pushed it toward the elevator. Chris looked back at his fat boss and gave him the finger as the door closed. As the elevator went up, he began thinking about how things got the way they were.

It had been his evident fault. He had always been the root of most of his problems. He had a knack for messing things up. He had gotten into a fight with a bunch of older kids back in high school. That was how he had met Martin.

Martin had bailed him out of more jams than he could count. Even after Chris's treatment, he was still looking out for him. After the incident at the apartment, Martin had come to him and tried to square things up.

It had taken over three weeks, but after his mother would not take him back, Chris realized he was stuck here in New York. He also knew he would need help.

Martin gave him the keys to the apartment. He told Chris he could live there rent-free. Maybe Martin had felt guilty for taking Chris's girlfriend away; nevertheless, it was something Chris had not expected, but he took it. He needed a place to stay; somewhere free was much better than cheap.

Roxy and Martin lived together in a high-rise condo in Manhattan. The two of them had invited Chris to come over to talk, but he had rejected their invitation. He was not quite ready to see them together. He was still furious with both of them.

When the door to the elevator opened, Chris stepped out and then started to deliver the mail to the people in their offices.

Martin had not just stopped at giving him the apartment. He also put a good word into his workplace. That was how Chris got this job.

Chris remembered it was here Martin had started. Working in the mailroom, now he was upstairs with the big wigs. If Martin could do it, so could he. Chris thought to himself daily. That is if he did not mess it up first. He was already on bad terms with the boss and many other people in the mailroom.

"Hey! Mail boy!" someone shouted at him as he walked down the hallway.

Chris turned around with a look that could kill. One of the people had come out of their office and handed him a large box. The people on the upper floors treated the mail clerks like lower life forms. They never said thank you or addressed them by name. Chris hated all of them.

"This needs to go out tomorrow, first thing," the man said. Without waiting for a reply, he was back in his office, closing the door before Chris could say anything.

"Don't pay any attention to them," a female voice said.

"Hey, Andrea," Chris said.

He looked back at the elevator. She was walking his way. Andrea was one of the other male runners.

"I just finished my load; I heard you took the last one. Figured I would give you a hand," Andrea said.

Chris sighed a breath of relief. He could do with an extra pair of hands.

"Just don't tell the dough man," she said with a smile.

Chris liked her, not how she wanted him, which was evident to everybody. He still had feelings for Roxy, which he knew wouldn't be fair to Andrea if he returned her affection for him. The two got through the rest of the mail quickly.

"What are you doing this weekend?" Andrea asked him as they walked towards the exit.

"Have to look for another job," Chris lied.

He knew she wanted to ask him out again. She had asked numerous times. He had come up with an excuse every time.

"Rent is killing me, and these hours are not cutting it," Chris lied for the hundredth time.

Andrea nodded. "Well, see you Monday then," she said as she turned away.

Chris walked towards the bus stop. He couldn't stop thinking of Andrea besides his feelings for Roxy. He had no real reason for not going on a date with her. Most of the other guys in the mailroom would love it if she paid them the same attention, she showed him.

It was not like she was ugly. In fact, she was quite attractive. The thing was, she was black. Not that Chris had a problem with black women, but they had always intimidated him. The way they talked and how loud they could be at times.

Andrea had long jet-black hair and brown eyes and was quite thick all around but mainly around the hips and ass. He loved looking at her walk away. Her ass swayed just the right way. She had a nice pair of tits, too, not as big as Roxy, but there were not many women as developed as Roxy was in the chest area. He sat at the bus stop, looking at his phone, when a car pulled up.

"Get in," Andrea said.

"It's no big deal. The bus..." Chris began to say.

"It was not a question. Get in," Andrea said much louder the second time.

The other people at the bus stop stopped doing whatever they were doing to look at him. He knew what they were thinking. He must be stupid to pass up a car ride at this time. He got up from the seat and got into her car.

"Look. It isn't often I fall for a guy, so let's talk. What's up?" Andrea asked.

Chris quickly pulled on his seat belt. Her erratic driving made him nervous.

"Nothing. Just got out of a..." Chris began to say before she interrupted him.

"Don't even. I know all about that," Andrea said, cutting him off. "You left her and him in the same apartment. No goodbye, no nothing just up and left. If you did that to me, with a guy like him my legs would be in the air touching the ceiling too," she said, narrowly missing a car.

"Well..." he began to say.

"No well anything," she interrupted. "Did you? Or did you not leave?" she said with authority. She looked at him.

"Yes, but..." he began to say again.

"But nothing! Soon as you left, you gave up all rights to what you had, with both. And if I am not wrong, did you or did you not get with another woman?" Andrea asked.

Chris nodded as he held the bar over his head as she narrowly missed another car.

"Now, you just want to waltz back into their lives after months of being away and pick up where you left off. Motherfucker please!" Andrea said, zigzagging in and out of traffic.

Chris had not seen this side of her, and it was unpleasant. At work, she was mild-mannered, polite, and always willing to help. Now she seemed angry and ready to rip his head off.

"Look, I don't usually get all mad like this. But I really like you for some reason. I still don't know why maybe it's that Eminem look; you got going on. But I do. And I have seen you checking my ass out. Plus, I know you have a thing for big boobs, and I got them," Andrea said, letting go of the steering wheel and squeezing her breasts with both hands. "So, this is how it is going to go," she said, pulling up to the subway station.

Andrea stopped the car and then turned to face him. She looked profoundly serious. He felt slightly uncomfortable, but she turned him on simultaneously.

"Tomorrow night you will meet me here around ten, we will go out, my treat. We can see where this thing leads us, if there is nothing then, we go our separate ways no harm no foul, but if there is something, then we go from there," Andrea said.

"Okay," Chris nodded. Part of him wanted to tell her no, and the other wanted him to take a chance.

"Again, it was not a question," Andrea said.

Chris got out of the car and headed down into the subway. He began to wonder what he had gotten himself into, what would happen if he did not show up. He could say something came up. He got onto his train and sat there pondering. His phone rang.

"Hello," he answered.

"Hey, Chris," Martin said.

"Hey," he replied.

"How is it going?" Martin asked.

"What do you want?" Chris responded.

Chris had no patience for his old friend. Even though Martin had done a lot for him, he still hadn't forgiven him. He knew it was out of guilt, more than anything, that he couldn't move on from their betrayal. Maybe Andrea was right. Perhaps this was his fault that this had happened.

"Fine. Let's get it out in the open. Roxy and I are thinking of getting married," Martin said.

The news hit Chris like a punch to the stomach. "You guys barely know each other," Chris said.

Which was a lie. They had known each other the whole time Chris and Roxy had dated. Plus, the amount of time he went away, now they lived together. A lot of people got married in shorter lengths of time.

"Well, it's a thought. It isn't in the books yet, but I thought you should know," Martin said.

"Well, I could do with a car, so if that guilty thing is still working. I will take a car, and we can call it even," Chris said bitterly.

"Fuck you. Call me back when you grow up," Martin said, hanging up.

Chris gripped the phone hard. He wanted to throw it, but without it, he would not have a way to be contacted if his boss had more hours for him.

The apartment felt empty now that it was just him. He popped a frozen dinner in the microwave and sat at the table. He remembered the times the three of them sat here eating dinner.

He knew Andrea was right; it was his fault. He did leave. At the time, he had thought Roxy would chase him. Roxy didn't come after him. She didn't even ask about him.

The more that he thought about it, why she would. They never really hit it off. They were put together on a blind date by some friends. Sure, they had an excellent time during those first few weeks, but then she lost her job, and he offered her to stay with him. After that, things went downhill fast.

Chris decided. He was going to go with Andrea. Maybe he could take his mind off them for a while. A night out of this quiet apartment might do him some good.

THE COLD AIR WAS BITING him as he stood outside the subway station, waiting for Andrea. She was very late. He was going to give her a few more minutes. Then he was going to go. He looked at his watch. It was thirty-five minutes after ten. A car raced to a stop right in front of him. A vehicle behind it beeped its horn.

"Beep that fucking horn, one more time," Andrea said, getting out of the car and walking towards the back of the vehicle. Chris ran and stopped her.

"What?" Andrea said as the car passed her. Chris smiled. "What are you smiling for?" she asked with a smile.

"You. You're so quiet at work," Chris said as she got back in the car. He got into the passenger seat.

"That's work, Andrea. Now you can see the real me. My parents told me to stick up for myself, cause no one else will. So..." she shrugged.

"Where are we going?" Chris asked.

"Some new nightclub. I heard about," Andrea said, shrugging.

Chris quickly put his seat belt on as she dashed in and out of traffic, barely missing some of the cars. He had never felt this nervous inside a vehicle before.

"Who taught you to drive?" he asked.

"No one," Andrea said with a smile. "I haven't had an accident yet."

"Yet being the key word," Chris said, holding on for dear life.

There was a line to enter the nightclub, but Chris lined up at the back. Andrea grabbed his hand firmly and began to pull him toward the front.

"Boy sometimes I wonder about you," Andrea said, shaking her head.

"Excuse me there is a line," A lady began to say.

"I know but..." Chris started to reply.

"Who are you talking to?" Andrea asked the lady.

"I was telling him, there is a line," the lady said.

"And I choose to ignore it," Andrea said.

The bouncer at the door looked in their direction. He walked towards them as they got to the front of the line. He shook his head and then folded his arms.

"Back of the line. Please," he said.

"No. Get Anthony please," Andrea said.

"I said back of the line," The bouncer said, ducking under the rope.

The large man approached Chris. Andrea stepped in front of Chris. She pushed Chris behind her and then looked up at the tall man.

"And I said, can you please get Anthony. I said it politely. I don't think you want me to..."

"Andrea!" a large black man said, coming from inside.

"Hey, Cuz," Andrea said.

"Let them in. That's my cousin," Anthony said.

The bouncer shook his head and opened the rope, letting them inside. Once they got inside the club, Andrea and her cousin hugged each other.

"What's up with your boys? Got to teach them respect," Andrea said.

"I'll talk to them, but you got to watch that attitude," Anthony said, walking them further into the club.

"Got me this far, hasn't it," Andrea said as they entered.

The club was full of people. Three floors with two massive dance floors. People were everywhere. Chris took it all in. He liked it.

"Enjoy yourselves," Anthony said with a smile. "I don't want any trouble!" He pointed at Andrea.

They walked over to one of the tables. Andrea took her short coat off. Revealing a short purple dress that stuck to her curves like a second skin.

"Glad you like it," Andrea said, catching him staring at her deep cleavage.

"Yeah, I do," Chris replied, looking away.

"Oh, you can stare all you like," Andrea said. "I didn't push these girls into this tight dress for nothing," she said, squeezing her massive tits together.

They looked around for a while, and then his eyes locked onto someone. He turned and looked at Andrea shaking his head.

"You knew," Chris said.

"Yup," Andrea said. "I am going to get us some drinks," she said, walking away.

The other lady walked up to the table and sat across from him.

"Hello Chris," Roxy said.

"Roxy," Chris replied, trying to sound uninterested.

"Don't," Roxy said, shaking her red hair. It was longer than before. He knew Martin had a thing for long hair.

"What?" he replied.

"That macho thing you try to pull. Don't do it," Roxy said.

"Oh, I am glad to hear. It's not something new," Andrea said, returning.

"Hey, Andrea," Roxy said, hugging Andrea.

"Hey, girlie," Andrea said, returning the hug.

"Heard you got into it with Jeon outside," Roxy said, smiling.

"Yeah, that mother..." Andrea said before calming herself down.

"What am I going to do with you?" Roxy said with a smile.

"Same thing everyone else does. Leave me the fuck alone," Andrea replied.

Roxy smiled. Chris looked stunned. "Yeah, me and your ex, go way back. You're not the only one that has had a fall out with their best friend."

"When Andrea told me about some guy at work she liked, that had a chip on his shoulder. I knew it had to be you. So, I told her to bring you here," Roxy said.

"Now, you two done?" Andrea asked.

"I am. Maybe you can help him grow up and realize people eventually go their separate ways," Roxy said, giving Andrea another hug.

"Do your thing. I got this," Andrea said.

Andrea looked at Chris, who felt betrayed even further. He thought this was supposed to be a night for the two of them. Not for her to bring him to his ex's job to be embarrassed.

"So, what else do you have in store. Are we going to Martin's new apartment?" Chris asked.

"First off, drop the attitude I am the one with the attitude. It does not look good on you," Andrea said. "Second, No. I brought you here so that we could have a good time together. And so, you can see that eventually friends do go their separate ways. Maybe you and Martin had the best friendship either of you will ever have, but if it's over it's over."

That was a hard thing for Chris to accept. Even though Martin had betrayed him, they had been through a lot together. Deep down, Chris wanted to forgive him. But he didn't know how.

"You going to ask me to dance?" Andrea asked. Chris snapped back to reality.

"Yeah, but I am not good at it," he said, standing up.

"We will see," Andrea said.

Andrea took his hand and then down to one of the dance floors. She put her big ass firmly against him and pushed it firmly back on him. Chris just stood there. Her ass was grinding up and down around on his dick, turning him on. She then took his hands and glided them over her hips and thighs. He started to push forward onto her.

"Well, someone wants to say hello," Andrea said, grinding her ass backward harder.

Chris was getting harder by the second. Andrea moved his hands upwards over her stomach and just below her tits. She quickly turned around, facing him. Wrapping her arms around his neck, they looked at each other face to face as they got close.

"How am I doing?" Chris asked.

Andrea smiled at him. "Not too bad for a white boy," she said. Rubbing her leg between his, pushing her thigh up against his dick. "Not too bad at all."

"May I cut in?" Roxy said.

"Sure, go at it, girl," Andrea said. She walked away, leaving Chris and Roxy to dance alone.

Chris looked over at Andrea. She was talking to someone. When the light hit the person, he could see it was Martin.

"Don't worry, I think she can handle herself," Roxy said.

"Those two would make a great couple," Chris said with a smile.

He thought of the two of them together. Her attitude mixed with his take-no-prisoners, never-back-down mentality. It would be like two bulls going at it.

"Yeah, it would be fun to see," Roxy replied.

The two of them talked for a while. Roxy told him that liking Martin and finally getting with him was something she had always wanted from the moment she moved in.

Eventually, they both agreed that they had a good time. But it was over. They walked over to the table where Martin and Andrea were sitting. The two didn't look like they were arguing, but it didn't look like they were talking much, either.

"You two sorted out now?" Martin asked.

"Yeah, we are good," Chris said.

"Good," Andrea said. "Because I am tired," she said, getting up.

"One thing," Chris said as he nodded toward Martin.

The two of them walked outside.

"I don't want to be friends anymore," Chris said first. Martin nodded. "I can't see the two of you together, not right now anyway. Maybe one day I might be able to, but I doubt it."

"That's understandable," Martin said.

Chris reached into his pocket for the apartment keys. He tried to hand them over to Martin.

"No keep it. I didn't give it to you out of guilt. You were the one that picked it out when we first moved up here. So, it's yours." Martin said, pushing the keys back. Chris nodded.

The girls came out of the club. They were standing just a few feet away from them. The two men looked over at the women.

"She is a real lady, a bit rough around the edges," Martin said with a slight nod. "But she will keep you out of trouble."

"Or get me into it," Chris said.

"No. You need someone like her," Martin said. "For too long you have been the person to get yourself into trouble, now you can be the person to keep someone else out of it."

Chris nodded with a smile. "You're always looking out for me, aren't you?" Chris said, shaking his head. He finally figured it out. "You set this all up, didn't you?"

"I have always been there, hard to break a habit," Martin shrugged. "I knew it was at its end. So had to find someone else to take over. And well I knew about her, and..." Martin said.

"You can stop now," Chris said, interjecting as he walked away. "Thanks, Thanks for everything. I will be good."

The two nodded at each other, and then Chris and Andrea walked toward her car.

"SO, THIS IS THE FAMED apartment," Andrea said as she entered.

"Yeah, this is it," Chris said, throwing the keys on the table.

"It's much bigger than my place," Andrea said, walking into the kitchen.

"Two bedrooms upstairs," he said.

"Are you hinting at something?" Andrea said, turning to face him.

"No, just was saying..." he began to say before she kissed him.

"Too bad. Cause I was going to ask where they were," Andrea said.

They locked lips again. Andrea grabbed onto him and pulled him onto her. He loved how aggressive she was.

"Right up here," Chris said, racing up the stairs.

They went into his old room. Andrea pushed him down onto the bed. She quickly took off his jeans.

"Definitely not too bad for a white guy," Andrea said, taking his dick into her mouth.

"Fucking hell!" Chris exclaimed as she took all seven inches into her mouth easily. Her head bounced furiously on his cock. "Oh, my fucking god!" he said, looking down at her head bob up and down without stopping. "Fuck, that feels so fucking good!" he said, gripping the sheets as she sucked the life out of him.

Her hand went down to his balls, then began squeezing and massaging them as she sucked him. She hadn't stopped sucking him. She didn't even stop to take a breath. He couldn't last any longer.

"Fuck I am going to cum," Chris shouted. She started to go faster, which he didn't even think was possible. "I'm cumming fuck I'm cumming!" he repeated repeatedly. As he began to cum in her mouth.

"Sorry," Chris said as she finished swallowing all his cum.

"For what?" Andrea said, kissing him.

"Cumming so fast," he said.

Andrea shrugged. "It happens. It just means you got to please me now before I please you again," she said.

Chris reached down her top, squeezing her massive tits. They were soft and firm. He pressed and pinched the nipples. She moaned lightly.

"While that does feel great, I was thinking of something lower," she pulled up her skirt, revealing her black thong.

Chris took the hint. He pulled it down quickly and began to lick and finger her. She was already wet. He was good at this. He had a lot of practice from nights of not getting Roxy off. Andrea was already close to cumming. She began rolling her hips on his tongue. Her legs spread wider as he increased his pace,

"Fuck, you got a tongue on you," Andrea said aloud.

She reached down, grabbing the back of his head. Her long nails dug into his hair. She held him right up against her dripping pussy.

"Right there, right fucking there," Andrea yelled again.

He licked faster, flicking his tongue all over and around her clit. Then he began to suck on it, pushing two fingers deep inside her. He finger fucked her hard. Slamming his fingers into her repeatedly.

"Damn boy you know what you're fucking doing," Andrea said, grabbing her boob with her free hand.

He grabbed her waist and began pushing his finger deeper into her. Slowly he inserted another finger into her ass.

"Oh fuck," Andrea said as she tried to get away from him.

He began to finger her ass and pussy slowly while eating her out. Her body was trembling and shaking with every touch. Her legs locked themselves around him.

"Fuck you, you pussy eating mother fucker," Andrea began swearing as she tried to control herself. Her back began to arch as the first orgasm crashed over her. "Don't stop!" she said as another came; he began to slide his finger into her ass deeper. Another one came following the last. "Enough!" she screamed out loud, pushing him away.

Andrea was sweating hard; her black hair was a mess and hung off her face. Chris was sweating too. His face was covered with her pussy fluids. He had never done anything like that before. Roxy had always shied away from him, putting a finger inside her ass.

"Stand up," Andrea ordered.

Andrea took off her dress, revealing a black bra. She quickly unhooked it. Then knelt in front of him. She grabbed her big boobs and slapped them around his dick. He began fucking upwards into her tits. He squeezed her dark brown nipples. Watched his white cock, poke in and out of the top of her boobs.

"Fuck yeah. Push them together tighter," Chris said.

"Nu-uh," she said as she pulled them apart.

"I want to fuck this," Andrea said as she pulled him towards the bed.

Andrea spread his legs wide open as he lay on his back. She climbed on top with her back to him. She buried his white dick inside her. She bounced back and forth on it. He had the perfect view of her big ass bouncing on his cock. She started going faster and faster. Her ass was a blur bouncing on his dick.

"Like the view of your white cock going inside me don't you." Andrea said back at him.

Chris was speechless, trying to concentrate on not cumming. Andrea bent forward, almost laying down between his legs, her ass raised in the air and back down on his dick repeatedly.

He reached forward with both hands grabbing a firm grip on her ass. It shook and twitched between his hands. He pushed it up and down and then gave it a hard slap. It jiggled as he slapped it.

"She might beat me in the boob department, but she could never beat me in riding a dick," Andrea said as she rode him harder.

Chris felt she would ride him hard enough to tear his dick right off.

"Fuck I am cumming," he said.

Andrea quickly rolled off him and spun around. Taking his dick between her boobs again. His cum shot upwards, splashing on her tits. She pushed her tits to her face and licked his cum off them.

She climbed up the bed and then lay down next to him. "As first dates go. How bad was it?" Andrea laughed. He kissed her. "Okay, not so bad," she said as they laughed.

LATER THAT NIGHT, CHRIS got up. He left her lying there on his bed. He walked into Martin's old room. Everything was gone. He stood in the empty space, remembering everything the two had been through together.

Then he saw something outside the window. He walked towards the window. A smile filled his face. Martin waved up at him. Chris waved back. Martin nodded as he got back into his car and raced away.

"What are you doing?" Andrea asked.

"Nothing. Thinking about turning this room into a studio. I always wanted to make my own music, maybe become a DJ, or something," Chris nodded.

"Come back to bed," Andrea said, smiling.

The End.

Don't miss out!

Visit the website below and you can sign up to receive emails whenever Alexander Martin publishes a new book. There's no charge and no obligation.

https://books2read.com/r/B-A-NVEDB-VOZZE

BOOKS 2 READ

Connecting independent readers to independent writers.

Also by Alexander Martin

Adventures With Married Women
Adventures With Married Women: Game Day
Adventures with Married Women: Closing The Store
Adventures With Married Women: Night Flight
Adventures with Married Women: Football Mom
Adventures With Married Women: Gym Heroics
Adventures With Married Women: More Testing
Adventures With Married Women: Further Down the Rabbit Hole
Adventures With Married Women: Other Men's Property
Adventures With Married Women: Never A Dull Moment
Adventures With Married Women: Birthday Treats
Adventures With Married Women: The Wedding Invitation
Adventures With Married Women: Unexpected Invitation
Adventures With Married Women: Dinner Date
Adventures With Married Women: Smarter Decisions
Adventures With Married Women: New Batch

Best Friend's Mom
Best Friend's Mom: Work Life Balance
Best Friend's Mom: Dinner Date
Best Friend's Mom: Moving Out

Black Lake

Black Lake: The Chains That Bind

Crime Does Pay

Follow The Rules

Family Business

Crossroads

Crossroads: Time Waits For No One

From Prude to Whore

From Prude to Whore: Sister Marci

From Prude To Whore: Sister Marci Finale

Gilf Adventures

Gilf Adventures: The Break

GILF Adventures: Anniversary Date: Leslie

Hall Pass

Hall Pass: Another Man's Treasure

Mistakes Were Made
Mistakes Were Made: The Night Out
Mistakes Were Made: Opportunity Gained
Mistakes Were Made: Challenge Accepted

Office Relations
Office Relations: The New Boss
Office Relations: Helpful Boss
Office Relations: The H.R. Meeting
Office Relations: Releasing Tension

Simple Women
Simply Jennifer
Simply Ms. J

The Condo Club
The Condo Club: The Blonde
The Condo Club: The Secretary
The Condo Club: The Maintenance Worker
The Condo Club: The Winning Team

Standalone
A Better View
A Different Kind Of Summer

A Dish Served Cold
A New Direction
Snowed In
A New Helen
Bull By The Horns
A New Life
A New Look
A Simple Smile
Wife Swap
Mother's Daughter
A Star Returns
The Other Woman
Token Thanksgiving
A Trip To Remember
A View To Remember
Catching Up
Chance Encounter
Actions and Consequences
Piece by Piece
Reality Check
Friendly Advice
Getting The Grade
Business Date
Playing The Game
The Good Wife
No Risk, No Reward
Bride To Be
No More Vanilla
The Perfect Wife
Exceptional Circumstance
Never Too Old
Parents, Teachers and Coaches
All in the Family

The Feel of Her
The Work Wife
Reunions
Bad Decisions
Change Happens
Behind Blue Eyes
Christmas At Joes
Being Neighborly
Best Friend's Girl

Watch for more at https://alexander-martin.medium.com/lists.

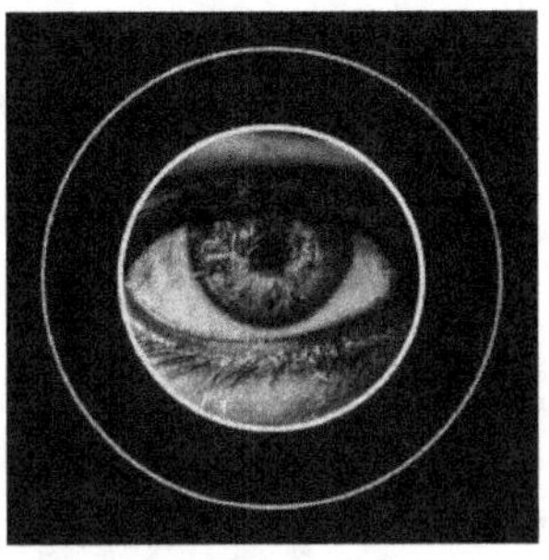

About the Author

I write long and detailed stories that are mostly interracially motivated. I have never been able to write small stories well; I like the how, when, and where. Most of my female characters are independent and strong-minded. I hope most of my readers will leave comments and tell me what they think so I can improve.

Read more at https://alexander-martin.medium.com/lists.

www.ingramcontent.com/pod-product-compliance
Lightning Source LLC
Chambersburg PA
CBHW061627130726
47996CB00003B/1154